WATTERS · LEYH · DOZERDRAWS · LAIHO

LUMBERJANES™

INDOOR RECESS

BOOM! BOX™

LUMBERJANES Volume Thirteen, December 2019. Published by BOOM! Box, a division of Boom Entertainment, Inc.

For information regarding the CPSIA on this printed material, call: (203) 595-3636 and provide reference #RICH – 872247.

BOOM! Studios, 5670 Wilshire Boulevard, Suite 400, Los Angeles, CA 90036-5679. Printed in USA. First Printing.

ISBN: 978-1-68415-450-0, eISBN: 978-1-64144-567-2

THIS LUMBERJANES FIELD MANUAL BELONGS TO:

NAME:________________________

TROOP:________________________

DATE INVESTED:________________________

FIELD MANUAL TABLE OF CONTENTS

LUMBERJANES FIELD MANUAL

For the Intermediate Program

Tenth Edition • January 1985

Prepared for the

Miss Qiunzella Thiskwin Penniquiqul Thistle Crumpet's

CAMP FOR  

"Friendship to the Max!"

A MESSAGE FROM THE LUMBERJANES HIGH COUNCIL

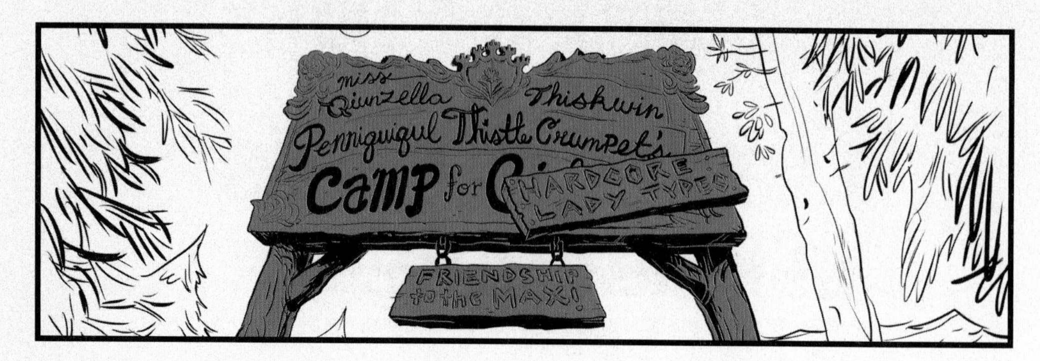

You may find—especially if you have proven yourself to be a stalwart and thoughtful friend—that the people you hold dearest value your ideas and advice. And this is a wonderful thing. It shows that you have been there for them in times of need, and that you are able to consider and understand the wishes of others: these are qualities which we of the Lumberjanes High Council commend in our scouts, and which the Lumberjanes pledge specifically asks of us all.

However, at a certain point, even the most empathetic person will find themselves worn out and disheartened, and at a loss for what to say. You've gone to the well of your love and care, and found it dry, with nothing left to give right now.

This may make you worry that you've let your friends down, or that there is something the matter with you, but this isn't the case at all. Wells run out when we demand too much of them, and if we drink them dry, it is not the well's fault. We all need time and space to rest and recover: to replenish our stores and rejuvenate our hearts. It may seem counterintuitive, or even hard-hearted, but the best thing you can do is step back.

You have become used to speaking, and to offering advice. You are used to knowing answers. You may even fear that this is the only way you can be helpful, although this is never the case. The cure for this fear is listening. Start small, and listen to yourself. What do you need? How can you help yourself reconnect to the parts of you that are worn out and tired? What will help them flourish and grow again?

Then, when you're feeling a touch less frustrated, consider setting yourself free from expectations. Listen to your friends the next time you see them, rather than offering any advice. It may be that a simple receptive ear will already be of great comfort to them, even if you aren't able to help solve their problems.

Finally, try stepping beyond. We High Councillors find that nature is often a wonderful place to venture outside of yourself and your own worries. So, try hiking into the woods, and listen to the eminent silence that will surround you there. Let its stillness and fullness wash over you, and let it leave your body ringing with a sense of tranquility and activity, ease and ambition, leisure and industry. All of these together compose the natural world, and each of us. Let the cool rain replenish your well, and breathe deep. Your self will flow back to you.

THE LUMBERJANES PLEDGE

I solemnly swear to do my best
Every day, and in all that I do,
To be brave and strong,
To be truthful and compassionate,
To be interesting and interested,
To pay attention and question
The world around me,
To think of others first,
To always help and protect my friends,
~~[illegible]~~
And to make the world a better place
For Lumberjane scouts
And for everyone else.

THEN THERE'S A LINE ABOUT GOD, OR WHATEVER

Written by
Shannon Watters & Kat Leyh

Illustrated by
Dozerdraws

Colors by
Maarta Laiho

Letters by
Aubrey Aiese

Cover by
Kat Leyh

Designer
Marie Krupina
Associate Editor
Sophie Philips-Roberts
Series Editor
Dafna Pleban
Collection Editor
Jeanine Schaefer

*Special thanks to **Kelsey Pate** for giving the Lumberjanes their name.*

Created by Shannon Watters, Grace Ellis, Noelle Stevenson & Brooklyn Allen

LUMBERJANES FIELD MANUAL

CHAPTER FORTY-NINE

I have an update for the legions of you who've been asking...
MESS HALL
...and unfortunately the storm is STILL showing no signs of stopping...

Look, I know everyone is feeling a little COOPED UP here in the Mess Hall, but unfortunately the Arts and Crafts barn is still recovering from a...

...GLITTER-related incident...

...and that leaves us with ONLY the Mess Hall to wait out the rain.

I have a list of approved indoor acti--
HEADS UP!

WAH!
SMACK
YO MY BAD! SORRY, JEN!
A crackerjack pitch, scout! But as Jean was saying, see your counselor for a list of APPROVED indoor activities and use the sign-up sheets by the door!
We're all gonna make the BEST of this!
WE'VE ALREADY BEEN IN HERE FOREVER!
It's been... 17 minutes.
Yeaaaah...but doesn't this storm seem a touch ODD? Like, it's been going a LONG TIME, right?
OH! OH OH! Like maybe... supernaturally long?!
YES! Yes, we should check ou--
APRIL!

I can actually HEAR the future rule breaking from whatever it is you're discussing and NO!
How did you--
There is a perfectly normal--
BUT J--
bup bup bup! --NORMAL but still DANGEROUS storm out there.
I need you girls to PROMISE me...
SIGH
Promise me, you'll stay inside!
We promise!
Great! There are LOTS of fun, safe, EDUCATIONAL and dry activities to choose from! You'll see!

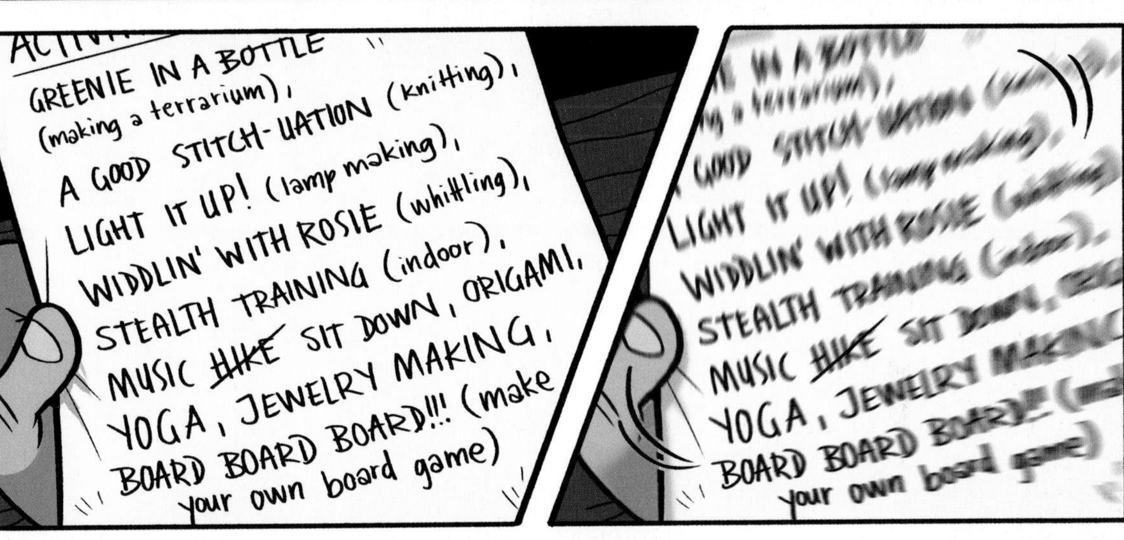
GREENIE IN A BOTTLE (making a terrarium),
A GOOD STITCH-UATION (knitting),
LIGHT IT UP! (lamp making),
WIDDLIN' WITH ROSIE (whittling),
STEALTH TRAINING (indoor),
MUSIC HIKE SIT DOWN, ORIGAMI,
YOGA, JEWELRY MAKING,
BOARD BOARD BOARD!!! (make your own board game)

SHAKE
SHAKE
SHAKE
TAP
TAP
TAP

UUGH!

OH! I know what we could do!

We're stuck in the Mess Hall, right?

KITCHEN
NO CAMPERS BEYOND THIS POINT!
Let's go on a **snack run**!

I think Jen emphatically wants us to not break any rules today...let's give the ol' girl a thrill and actually listen?
Sorry, Rip. But hey, some of these activities look right up your alley!
I'm sure we can find something interesting to do!

I'm gonna go to the jam session!
I think I'll try knitting...

C'mon, Rip, you and I can find something to do together!

Jewelry making?
Mehhhh...

Oof!

Sorry! We're making room for the board games!

OOF!
Room for two more?
Yeah! Come and join us!

Great!
Eeeeesh...

SNA
ACKS

SNACK
RUN

April?

Um, yours doesn't look quite like a frog, but...

...it DOES look good enough to eat! Haha!

AH!

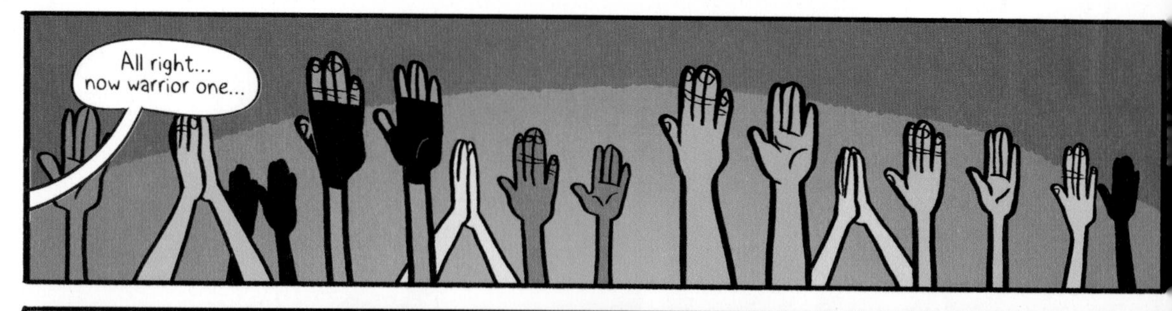
All right... now warrior one...

Good...

Now bend down...

Excellent...

...and into downward dog...

SNACK RUN!!
Breathe...

Concentrate on your breathing...
pssst
FOCUS, Brain!
PSST! Ripley!

Brain?

SNACK RUN!
YEAH!
SSH!
Ripley?
NO CAMPERS BEYOND
Hmm, we're going to need some kind of distrac--
NO CAMPERS BEYOND THIS
Hey.
AH!

I thought I'd find you over here. Snack run?
Yeah!
I'm in.

Weren't you looking forward to the music "hike"?
Yeah, well, there would have been ROOM for everyone if it was outside, but instead everyone is poorly tuning on top of each other. I had to get outta there.

NO CAMPERS BEYOND THIS POINT!
I was just saying, we'll need a distrac--
If you play ONE MORE B#--

NO CAMPERS BEYOND THIS POINT!
I can't help it!
YOUR SLIDE KEEPS **BONKING** ME ON THE BACK OF MY HEAD!
Girls, we can move Jocelyn over by Mikki!

There's no room! Mikki's TUBA takes up all the space!
All instruments are WELCOME, Jocelyn!
NO CAMPERS BEYOND THIS POINT!

THEN WHY COULDN'T I BRING MY MARIMBA?!
BECAUSE IT'S THE SIZE OF A TABLE, KIM!

Girls! Settle down!
WE CAN'T **ALL** PLAY THE GLOCKENSPIEL, HEATHER!
Jo?

Something wrong?
I lost-- OHMYGOSH!
click
click
click

YOU MADE BUBBLES A BUBBLES HAT?!

It's the cutest thing I've ever seen! You're getting really good at this!
Thanks, Jo!
click
click
click

I find it very very very calming.
click
click
click

Jo! Jo! Oh--and Molly too!

Perfect!

Come with me! Come with me! I need your help with something!
Oh, hi, Emily! Help with what?

I'm creating a board game...for the "Board, Board, BOARD" badge? I've been working on it for a while and it is **EPIC!**

Now I need players for a trial run!

Sure!
SWEET LESLIE SCOTT THANK YOU!
I'm in.

I've been having trouble finding volunteers...
RULES
RULES
Sneak
sneak
Sneak
GASP!

BUNS
KEEP SHUT AT ALL TIMES!

TEMPTATION...

THUMBS UP!

Did you find anything Ri--!!!

"...I think the kids are getting cabin fever."

...sheesh, it's just more storage.

Lame.
But Mal!

Now you can say you've seen a jar of mayo the size of a sturdy toddler!
MAYO
Hahaha!

Ew.
HEY!

LOOK WHAT I FOUND!

Oooo, now THIS is what I'm talking about!

SECRET TUNNEL!
LET'S CHECK IT OUT!!
We can't! We promised Jen--

It's okay! We're still inside!

That's... technically true!

Just for a bit, though...

"...better than being in that overcrowded Mess Hall!"
Hey! Jo and Molly agreed to play! We can get started!

Welcome to *Penterra!*
My multi-tiered, world-building and conquest strategy game!
You all start off as rulers of your lands:
The Iron Hills!
Gullyglen!
Bloomeria!
Timbershins!
aaand Purple Town!
(I ran out of name ideas)
Now, let me start by explaining your Resource Cards and Export Tokens...

25 MINUTES LATER...
...Also, no two Expansion Cards of the same color can touch, BUT if you get enough Engineer Credits you can build a bridge, OR--and this is where the multi-tiers come in--a staircase...

Oh! Here's a fun thing I forgot, everyone gets a Rogue card but only ONE of them is genuine and so only one player can steal, but ANOTHER player can take it if they guess who has it, OR they have three Knights--

Waterways! I haven't even gotten into the waterways yet! Now, there's a lot of algebra used with navigating the various bodies of water--
ARGH!

OH MY DAD! CAN WE JUST **PLAY** ALREADY?!

Yeah, Emily, we have our rules sheets if we need to know anything else!
Let's do this!
RULES

I rolled a one! I go first!

WAH!

MAL?!

I'm fine, I walked into that tree root and it felt...vaguely creepy...

We must be WAY underground! How far do you think it goes?
And WHY? Why is there a tunnel in our kitchen?
GIANT MOLE, no, **GIANT RABBIT!**

I wanna see a giant rabbit **SO BAD!**

I think a giant rabbit is pretty unlikely, Rip...
Aaaw...
skitter
skitter

will co…

The u… It he… appeara… dress f… Further… Lumbe… to have… part in… Thiskv… Hardc… have… them…

…HE UNIFORM

…should be worn at camp …events when Lumberjanes …n may also be worn at other …ions. It should be worn as a … the uniform dress with …rrect shoes, and stocking or …

…out grows her uniform or … …her Lumberjane. …a she has … her … her

The … yellow, short sl… emb… the w… choose… slacks, … made o… out-of-dc… green bere… the colla… Shoes ma… heels, rou… …ings or socks shou… …with the shoes or wit… the uniform. Ne… …s, bracelets, or other jewelry do … belong with a Lumberjane uniform.

HOW TO WEAR THE UNIFORM

To look well in a uniform demands first of … uniform be kept in good condition—clean … pressed. See that the skirt is the right length for your own height and build, that the belt is adjusted to your waist, that your shoes and stockings are in keeping with the uniform, that you watch your posture and carry yourself with dignity and grace. If the beret is removed indoors, be sure that your hair is neat and kept in place with an inconspicuous clip or ribbon. When you wear a Lumberjane uniform you are identified as a member of this organization and you should be doubly careful to conduct yourself in a way that will show everyone that courtesy and thoughtfulness are part of being a Lumberjane. People are likely to judge a whole nation by the selfishness of a few individuals, to criticize a whole family because of the misconduct of one member, and to feel unkindly toward an organization because of the

The unifor… helps to cre… in a group. … active life th… another bond… future, and pr… in order to b… Lumberjane pr… Penniquiqul Thi… …ore Lady Types, but m… …s will wish to have one. They can either b… …uniform, or make it themselves from materials available at the trading post.

LUMBERJANES FIELD MANUAL

CHAPTER FIFTY

MESS HALL

Your turn, Diane!

Sigh.

I got...a stick.
No, it's a building material.
Sweet, Diane!

Building is SO FUN...
Are those...

...HOW DO YOU HAVE **ACTUAL MOVING** WIND TURBINES?!
...it's the BEST part of this game!
It's ONE of the best parts of the game...

Here you go!

Aaand, since it's your FOURTH dowel...

...ah ha!

Ta da!
BING!

Purple Town's first structure!
Yippee.

Don't worry, it's a great first step...

Hey! What else can I do on my turn?!
Do you want to Trade?

If you want more building supplies, I'll Trade for...I dunno...your water tokens.

Fine, whatever, okay now I want to build--
Sorry, Diane, you can't Build, Trade, then Build again! That would be anarchy!

And for MY turn I'm going to...

CONTEST THE BORDER!
GASP!

Double gasp!

That's right! Jo has three UNOCCUPIED expansion cards on my border...

Which means...

YEAH! That land belongs to ME now!

WOW! What a **MOVE,** Hes!

Get ready for Hes of The Iron Hills, RULER OF ALL PENTERRA!
I will be a fair and just ruler.
You think you stand a chance against Gullyglen: The City of Tomorrow?
Lemme see this dumb thing...
These nerds are going DOWN!

Venture deep in this forest and what will you find?
Oh, ha-rdcore ladies of e-ver-y kind!
Say, HEY, Lumberjanes' WAY!
Show me the WAY!
The Lumberjanes' WAY!
The Lumberjanes' w-- what was that?

I thought I heard... it sounded like skittering or something...

H-how far do you two want to explore down here, anyway?
Aw, Mal, I don't wanna head back yet! We've barely encountered any tall tales to tell everyone back at the Mess Hall!
I just think we should have a plan.

You okay, Mal? Are you scared?
What? No, I'm just...aware.

'Cause you KNOW you got ME here, right? I'll protect us from any unusually sized rodents, or whatever!
I'm FINE, April, really!

You want to carry the flashlight for a while?
I guess if you want a break...
Hey! Check this out!

Glowy goo!

Watch!
Oooo!
WHOOOA!
ha ha ha ha
huff huff Okay...
that was fun...but...

We should probably head back now.
AWWW
Mal, you're RIGHT!

If we go back now, we'll still have enough activity time left to grab the others and show them this place!

I bet this is science! Jen loves science!

I bet MOLLY would think it was pretty cool too!

It would be so romantic! Surrounded by beautiful, softly glowing fung--

--oof
THUMP
Uuuuh...

I don't remember passing any other tunnels...

How did this happen?!
We WERE running pretty fast...

BACK! WE SHOULD HAVE TURNED IT! NOW WE'RE LOST!
It's all right, Mal, we probably left tracks when we came through, we can--
Hey, guys?

See? I bet that was the one we came down! It's glowing!
SSSSS

SSSSSSSS
Wait, I hear that sound again!

SKIT
SKIT
SKIT
SSSSSSS

SKIT
SKIT
SKIT
Uh...

SKIT SKIT SKIT
AAAAAH!
MARIA SIBYLLA MERIAN! RUN!
"That was scary!"
SKIT SKIT SKIT

If you had rolled a five, you may have finally pulled ahead! Oh, well!
So close!
You're up, Molly.

Hmm, I got a Build card with a...

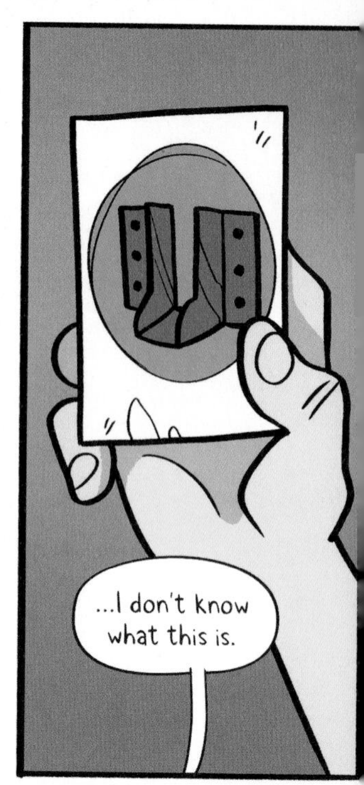
...I don't know what this is.

Oooh! A joist hanger! I need one of those!

Hey! Trash panda girl! I'll trade with you!
You 100% know my name, Artemis.

Molly, I will trade you my whole North Forest for your Build card!
Ooo, deal!

Thank you!
Thank YOU!
A SUDDEN CALAMITY! ROLL TO DECIDE YOUR NATURAL DISASTER!
I have no idea what's happening.
A what?
Oh that's a good one!

DINOSAUR RAIN!
Everyone has to discard one resource card, the dinosaurs ate them!
Haha!

Pst, small fry...

You're not doing so hot, what do you say we combine our resources against the two Lumbergeniuses over there?
I don't know... that feels so sneaky...
You'll just be helping me build up my city, it's not like it's against the rules, or anything.
Hmmm...

Here, I'll trade you some water tokens--they're not good for anything--for your Build cards.
Throw in your Knight, and we have a deal...

Ripley would love this part! I wonder which activity she ended up doing...

huff
huff
huff

We lost it!

That means WE'RE lost! And now we're lost with GIANT BU--
Don't say it! DON'T EVEN THINK IT.

Don't say what?
BUGS?

You're afraid of bugs?
Not AFRAID, I just don't like LOOKING at them!

All those legs, a never-ceasing number of legs--brrrr!

sigh

April, Ripley, don't worry! Everything's going to be okay!

What?
Nothing, it's just, three seconds ago you were kinda--
You were freaking out!

Well, I'm the oldest, so I'll get us out of here!

We'll keep heading uphill, eventually we'll HAVE to reach the surface!

What?
SSSSSSS

WAAAAH!
AAA--
HRK!
UPHILL! UPHILL! **UPHILL!**
"Do you have any threes?"

Go fish!

Excuse me! Do you mind if we use part of this table for our game?
Oh, sure...

THUNK!
Thanks!

There we go!

THUNK

I didn't really consider how... big this game could grow...
I'm done with my turn.
Molly, are you sure you don't want to *build* anything?
I did! I built a house.
Here in Timbershins we're all about trees! You're up, Barn!
haha...
HAHAHA!

THREE WATER TOKENS!

But that means...

--THE WATERWAYS ARE UNLOCKED!

But that's not all...because I also have...

GASP! THEY'RE THE ROGUE!

AND I control the waterways that run through all your lands...

The peaceful mayor of Bloomeria was a front all along for...

...the NOT peaceful
PIRATE CAPTAIN/
MAYOR OF
BLOOMERIA!

That was the raddest
combo move EVER!

...Upon reveal of the Rogue card
the Rogue may use their turn to...

...STEAL THREE
ASSETS?!
Good luck stopping
me without your
Knight! Ha HAH!

Y'all, my heart
is LITERALLY
pounding...
You...you...
tricked me? **YOU**
tricked **ME?!**

It's part of the game?
I...I...

My WORD, this is so exciting!
I really AM a bad influence! I'm so proud!

AAAAAAAAAAA!

will co

The u

It help

appeara

dress f

Further

Lumbe

to have

part in

Thisk

Hardc

have

them

E UNIFORM

hould be worn at camp

vents when Lumberjanes

may also be worn at other

ions. It should be worn as a

the uniform dress with

rect shoes, and stocking or

out grows her uniform or

her Lumberjane.

a she has

her

her

The

yellow,

emb

the w

choos

slacks,

made o

out-of-do

green bere

the colla

Shoes ma

heels, rou ... ings or

socks shou ... with the shoes or wi

the uniform. Ne ... es, bracelets, or other jewelry do

belong with a Lumberjane uniform.

HOW TO WEAR THE UNIFORM

To look well in a uniform demands first of ... uniform be kept in good condition—clean ... pressed. See that the skirt is the right length for your own height and build, that the belt is adjusted to your waist, that your shoes and stockings are in keeping with the uniform, that you watch your posture and carry yourself with dignity and grace. If the beret is removed indoors, be sure that your hair is neat and kept in place with an inconspicuous clip or ribbon. When you wear a Lumberjane uniform you are identified as a member of this organization and you should be doubly careful to conduct yourself in a way that will show everyone that courtesy and thoughtfulness are part of being a Lumberjane. People are likely to judge a whole nation by the selfishness of a few individuals, to criticize a whole family because of the misconduct of one member, and to feel unkindly toward an organization because of the

The unifor

helps to cre

in a group.

active life th

another bond

future, and pr

in order to b

Lumberjane pr

Penniquiqul Thi ... ore Lady

Types, but m ... will wish to have one. They can either bu ... uniform, or make it themselves from materials available at the trading post.

LUMBERJANES FIELD MANUAL

CHAPTER FIFTY-ONE

...Then I think the biggest flying bug was Meganeura, it was basically a dragonfly longer than your arm!
Oh! Oh! And Jaekelopterus! It was a GIANT SEA SCORPION THAT COULD GROW OVER EIGHT FEET! THAT IS SO. MANY. FEET!
...But that bug down here with US is like the Arthropleura, an ancestor of the millipede that could grow eight feet long AND almost two feet wide! So yeah, pretty close to the one in these tunnels...
But my ABSOLUTE FAVORITE prehistoric giant bug was probably--

Please. Ripley. No more.
...I was just gonna say "Mothra," and technically, April, she's not real...
That has not stopped LITERALLY ANYTHING that we've encountered this summer.

All the bugs I was talking about went extinct like...300 million years ago...
Hey! I bet it came over from that dimension the dinosaurs came from!
The giant creepy crawly in these tunnels must not have heard.

Let's talk about something else, huh, Rip? The bug stuff is freaking April out.

What about this glowing stuff? Why do you think it changes color?
I have a theory.

HAHAHA!
ZING!
:tickle:

Ooooo

I think it changes based on our emotions...
Like a mood ring? NICE.

I want to try and bring some back with us, I bet Jen and Jo would adore this stuff, those loveable nerds.

Hey, Mal! I bet you're wishing you'd stayed behind and done a **non**-underground activity with Molly, eh?
Hm? Oh, not really.

Hey! Look there!

I think...

...there's a light at the end of this tunnel!
It could be our way out!
Hey, what happened to the glow?
We're all still feeling feelings right?
Hang on...
The light is... getting closer...
I FOR SURE HAVE FEELINGS RIGHT NOW AT THIS MOMENT

SKITTER
SKITTER

AAAH!

trip

BOOF

LET'S G--

...Ripley?

Guys!
RI--

Up here!

Hurry!

Oh jeez oh jeez
oh jeez oh jeez

"You're all going DOWN!"

BWAAAHAHA! GONE ARE THE PEACEFUL WATERWAYS OF PENTERRA!

READY YOUR TERRITORIES FOR PILLAGING!
Hahaha! YES!
Dang, Barney.

Sorry, I'm getting extremely method as the Pirate-Rogue-Mayor I'm playing as now--
OF COURSE!

I should have included role playing from the START! Let's see...

...who wants a hat?!

The Iron Hills

Gullyglen
"City of Tomorrow."

Timbershins
I'm all set on hats. Thanks, though!

...aaaand gimme ooone second Diane...

PURPLE TOWN
Purple Town!

I'm not wearing this!
C'mon, get into the spirit of things!
Yeah, you should try to have some fun...this game is going to be over before you know it!

What's THAT supposed to mean...

Oh, nothing, just that this game might be over a lot quicker than y'all thought!

For example: ON MY NEXT TURN!

What?! No! I only JUST started my pirate empire!
Noooo!
Psh. Of COURSE one of you **rules nerds** would be the one to win!

I AM a rules nerd...

Diane! Whatever you do, take your time!
That's your big plan, Jo? Diane's gonna stall for time?

...I'm positively **shaking!**

Dearest Hester,
It ALMOST sounds like you're underestimating...

...my ability...

...to waste...

...t i m e.

I happen to know you can't spend more than a MINUTE coming up with your move, so--
But I CAN spend however long I need...

...on building
THIS stupid thing.

GASP! The Wibbly
Wobbly Power Tower!
What is that card
even FOR, though?

I'll admit, it was
one of my weirder ideas
I came up with when I
couldn't sleep...I meant
to remove it from
the deck...

If you can build
the tower, for however
long it stays STANDING,
you can have double
attack power with
your Warrior...

Whoops!
Better try again!
GUH!
CLATTER!
"You know what?"

I am DONE with these tunnels. Do you know why I came along in the first place? To feel LESS CRAMPED than when we were in the Mess Hall!
Well I did it for the snacks!
Yeah!
And that's ANOTHER thing! I didn't even get any snacks! I lost all my apples when we were running for our lives! SAD, SAD APPLES!
Oh! One sec...

Catch!

Aw, yes! Thanks!
Thanks, April!

Hey, Mal...what did you mean earlier when you said...you were glad you didn't stay back with Molly...?

What? I didn't say--

You guys aren't **breaking up** are you?
WHAT?! NO, we barely...we haven't--

sigh

All I MEANT was...Molly was looking forward to some quiet activity time. She wanted to learn how to knit. And I wanted to do something else! I'm glad we're both doing things we want to!

And although this is REALLY not what I had in mind...this is going to be **such a cool story** when I tell her about it later!

If we, y'know, ever get OUT of here...
We'll get you out of here, Mal!

In the NAME OF LOVE! In fact...
Oh jeez, April, c'mon

I see something! The tunnel...ends!

Does it look exit-esque?
I can't tell, it's too dark! But...

...there's water! It must be rain from the storm!!

You don't think it leads outside, though, do you?
I HOPE SO!

But we--

Mal! Do you still have the flashlight?

Yeah, let me find it...

click

B-b-b...
What is it? Please say it's not another flippin' GIANT BUG!

N-n-no.

BONES!

...Aaaand there!

Oh gosh darn me oh MY!

AARRRGH! Emily! DO SOMETHING ABOUT THIS.
Sorry, Hes! This is why we have beta testing! It's all about working out the bugs in a system!

THIS is a giant bug!

Agreed. I'm nerfing that particular card.
AH-HAH!

I've got you now, Hes!

You have more than TWO 3-story buildings on 3x2 agriculture land!
But--but it wasn't agricultural land when I built them!
That cow says otherwise!

The only thing you're allowed to do during your turn is bring your buildings up to code!

You said all that like it was interesting--hey!

Everyone is enjoying this game in different ways...

...there's nothing wrong with that.

Hahaha...

HAHAHA...

...You're RIGHT, Molly!
PURPLE TOWN

I got all caught up in the boring rules...

...I nearly forgot what it is I'M good at...

Uh?

WHOA!

...Making things
INTERESTING!

AHAHAHAHA!
"AAAAAH!"

CEMETERY! WE'RE UNDER A CEMETERY!
...CAN'T...DUST... THE STENCH... OF DEATH...OFF... MYSELF...

Wait!

They're...
tree roots!

Tree roots?
We have to be
near the surface!
That means--
Look!

There's light!
Is it...?

A WAY OUT!

AND LOOK!

The Mess Hall is RIGHT THERE!

WOO! YOU DID IT MAL!
WE MADE IT! LET'S GET OUT OF HERE!
No.

N--what?!

I don't think
we should...

WHY?!
What are you
talking about?!

We promised Jen
we wouldn't go outside
during this storm.

We have to find
another way out.
?!

will co…

The … It h… appear… dress f… Further… Lumbe… to have… part in… Thiskv… Hardc… have … them…

…HE UNIFORM

…should be worn at camp …events when Lumberjanes …n may also be worn at other …ions. It should be worn as a … the uniform dress with …rrect shoes, and stocking or …

… out grows her uniform or …ther Lumberjane. …insignia she has … her … her

The … yellow, short sl… emb… the w… choose… slacks, … made o… out-of-do… green bere… the colla… Shoes ma… heels, rou… …ings or socks shou… with the shoes or wi… the uniform. Ne…, bracelets, or other jewelry do … belong with a Lumberjane uniform.

HOW TO WEAR THE UNIFORM

To look well in a uniform demands first of … uniform be kept in good condition—clean … pressed. See that the skirt is the right length for your own height and build, that the belt is adjusted to your waist, that your shoes and stockings are in keeping with the uniform, that you watch your posture and carry yourself with dignity and grace. If the beret is removed indoors, be sure that your hair is neat and kept in place with an inconspicuous clip or ribbon. When you wear a Lumberjane uniform you are identified as a member of this organization and you should be doubly careful to conduct yourself in a way that will show everyone that courtesy and thoughtfulness are part of being a Lumberjane. People are likely to judge a whole nation by the selfishness of a few individuals, to criticize a whole family because of the misconduct of one member, and to feel unkindly toward an organization because of the

The unifor… helps to cre… in a group. … active life th… another bond… future, and pr… in order to b… Lumberjane pr… Penniquiql Thi… …ore Lady Types, but m… …es will wish to have one. They can either bu… the uniform, or make it themselves from materials available at the trading post.

LUMBERJANES FIELD MANUAL

CHAPTER FIFTY-TWO

BWAHAHAHA!
...Um

Diane, it, uh, is SUPER MEGA ULTRA against the rules to use magic to win--

I've done no such thing. Nothing's changed, like, really.

I've just made it more... interesting.
Ooo, she does have a point, Emily!

This IS pretty sweet.

Just 'til the end of the game?

I'm into it.

I guess if everyone's okay with it...

Yeah! Awesome! I have completely forgotten whose turn it is now...
MINE! Get ready to lose, ya losin' losers!

Okay, Ripley...

...we finally find a way OUT of this endless maze of--

--and you want to stay in here because...?
MANY-LEGGED HORRORS!
We promised!

We promised Jen we wouldn't go outside! Scout's honor and everything!

I'm PRETTY sure we already broke our promise, Rip. We're literally outside the Mess Hall.
But we're still inside... *something*! Jen said it was too dangerous in the storm!

THAT IS A TRUE FACT, BUT EMPHATICALLY ALSO IT'S DANGEROUS IN HERE! Jen wouldn't want us to stay **HERE**, either!
If Jen had seen..."many-legged horrors"...coming, I'm sure she would have made an exception.

But...

...I made a *promise*.

Rip, it's just not safe--

KRAK-A-DOOM!

KRK!
KRK!
KRK!
Whoa! Whoa! Whoa!
stumble

stumble

AAAAH!

OOF!

"Oh, WOW!"

Did anyone else SEE that? An old tree out there just got flippin' **obliterated** by lightning!

RAH! So that's it?! You get half my crops?!
Sorry, D, them's the rules!

All these **RULES!! THIS IS TOO COMPLICATED FOR ANYONE TO PLAY!**

WHAT ARE YOU **WRITING** OVER THERE!

I'm making a note about the danger of "rage-quitting" with this game.

Rage-quit? I'm gonna rage-**WIN!**
I'm not sure about that...

I think it's going to be down to those two.

This is it, Hes! I've got you cornered!
That's "Hes of the Iron Hills," and you ain't got NOTHIN'!
I have the farthest-reaching roads, my buildings are all up to code, tariffs paid, PLUS my city is ENTIRELY self-sufficient--

I am FOR REAL generating clean energy over here!
EXCEPT your easterly lands butt right up against my mountain range...
...or should I say VOLCANO?! HAHA!
Noooo! My quarries!

That was...

...exceedingly awesome, Diane.

Hey, wait, we're still enemies! You're going DOWN!
Actually, ABOUT that...

...um, I've been going through the resources that are left and you guys aren't going to like this but...

...NONE of you can win.
WHAT?!
"Whoa."

It's an ecosystem!
I thought maybe it was
just one giant millipede
that snuck through from
the dino dimension...

...speak of the devil!

WHOA! ALL THAT PRETTY GLOWING STUFF WAS ITS **POOP?!**

Or maybe it's...
Okay, girls, let's slooowly climb back up the way we--
EEEEE!

MOTHRA! IT'S MOTHRAS!

RIPLEY!

MAL!
AH!
OOF!

Ew ew ew ew

GASP

Oh, my Lisa Frank, it's adorable!
"What do you MEAN none of us can win?!"

Okay, so, this is one of the FIRST rules actually...

"Each player must have at least ONE of each Resource."...Then is goes on to list the seven types of building permits you can...(you know what that's not important.)

This is the TINIEST font...
Yeah, but I MUST have one of every...

...except for--

Right.

--TREES!!

I don't believe it...
Molly is hardly even PLAYING (no offense.)
Er, sorry, you guys...

So, wait, does that mean MOLLY wins?

Oh, goodness, no. Molly may have a tree monopoly, but those are the only Resource she DOES have! So by the same rule she can't win.

In that case...Emily...

...who DOES win?
That wasn't so bad.
You're too dang cute to be gross!
Ripley! Let go!
Noooo!
EEE!
OOF!
It's our "friend" and... HEY!

...AND IT'S BEEN PLUNDERING OUR PANTRY!
We should really tell the kitchen staff about this.

Rude!
No, that could be a good thing for us!

If it's going back and forth from the pantry, that's our way out of here!

Hey! You guys want to get back to the Mess Hall REALLY fast?

Oh, no...

C'mon, April! You were fine with the moth!
...no no no no NOPE.

This is the worst.

THIS IS THE BEST!
Just gotta hang on a little longer!

No, no, no.
No no no, this can't be right...
That's it! The entrance from the pantry!

MAYO

We made it...

Thanks for getting us back, Mal!

I saved some glowing bug poop to show Jen! Do you think she'll like them?!
Ripley, I'm not sure those things are--

GASP!
SKWIK

They're eeeeggs!

Uh oh.
SKWIK
"This is horrible!"
SKWIK
SKWIK
SKWIK
SKWIK

I've made a game that is LITERALLY impossible to win!

How did this happen?
There, there... here, have a hat.

I...kinda want to keep playing?
Yeah...

What do you say?! Let's see how far we can take this!
You're on!
Wh--really?
See? A few tweaks and--

What's that?
SKT
SKT
SKT
thud THUD THUD

SKT SKT SKT
KEEP SHUT AT ALL TIMES

KITCHEN
COOL OUTFITS!
WHAT HAVE YOU THREE BEEN **DOING?**
I HAVE SO MUCH TO TELL YOU!
I CAN SEE THAT!!!

MESS HALL
The girls will be thrilled this storm is finally over.
Those scouts had enough "inside time" to last them quite a while!
I better go tell them before they start to get a little out of control--
WHAM!
WAIT!

Are we allowed to leave, Jen?
NOD NOD
MESS HALL
WOO! THANKS JEN!
You're...welcome...
TO BE CONTINUED...

will co

The
It help
appeara
dress f
Further
Lumbe
to have
part in
Thiskv
Hard
have
them

HE UNIFORM

should be worn at camp
events when Lumberjanes
n may also be worn at other
ions. It should be worn as a
the uniform dress with
rrect shoes, and stocking or

out grows her uniform or
ther Lumberjane.
a she has
her
her

The
yellow, short sl
emb
the w
choos
slacks,
made o
out-of-d
green bere
the colla
Shoes ma
heels, rou
socks shou
the uniform. Ne
belong with a Lumberjane uniform.

HOW TO WEAR THE UNIFORM

To look well in a uniform demands first of
uniform be kept in good condition—clean
pressed. See that the skirt is the right length for your own height and build, that the belt is adjusted to your waist, that your shoes and stockings are in keeping with the uniform, that you watch your posture and carry yourself with dignity and grace. If the beret is removed indoors, be sure that your hair is neat and kept in place with an inconspicuous clip or ribbon. When you wear a Lumberjane uniform you are identified as a member of this organization and you should be doubly careful to conduct yourself in a way that will show everyone that courtesy and thoughtfulness are part of being a Lumberjane. People are likely to judge a whole nation by the selfishness of a few individuals, to criticize a whole family because of the misconduct of one member, and to feel unkindly toward an organization because of the

The unifor
helps to cre
in a group.
active life th
another bond
future, and pr
in order to b
Lumberjane pr
Penniquiqul Thi
Types, but m
can either bu
materials available at the trading post.

COVER GALLERY

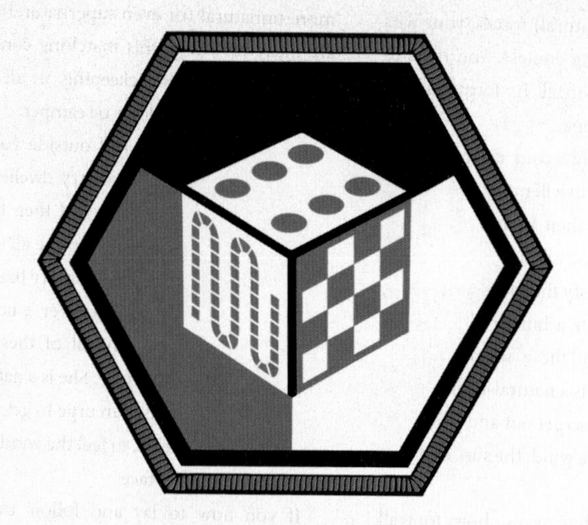

Lumberjanes "Out-of-Doors" Program Field

BOARD, BOARD, BOARD!

"Make Your Own Fun!"

From mancala to senet, backgammon to pachisi, checkers, reversi, mahjong, and even chess, board games have entertained human beings around the globe and across the centuries. Pieces, boards, and even dice for games have been found in ancient Egyptian tombs and carved into the marble floors of Roman ruins, just as they can be found today in the front hall closets and toy boxes of countless families just like yours.

As children, we learn through play. Imagination games train our creativity and our empathy, games like tag and hide-and-seek improve our problem-solving and coordination, and competitive sports teach us teamwork and improve our physical fitness. But board games have a special place in our hearts, both for the particular way that they can open up the doors to our imagination and for their availability, even on days when the rain pours or the snow piles up!

Board games, you may have noticed, grow with us. What you once found fun and exciting because it was a challenge will eventually become easy. In this way, board games can take us from color recognition and memory as toddlers, to matching and simple patterns as pre-schoolers, and into ever more complex ideas and concepts as we grow up. If you decide to sit down with your friends for an evening of board games now, you might be practicing skills like math and strategy, creative thinking, story telling, critical world-building, or even reading social cues! Through joy and exploration, you will learn the value of taking turns, of fairness, and of winning (or losing) graciously, all wrapped up in a brightly colored box, full of game tokens and dice.

Think about your favorite games. What is it about them that makes them fun to play? What keeps them exciting to return to, or have you started to invent new rules for more experienced players? If you were to create a board game of your own, what elements of your favorite games would you want to include? What type of story would you like your game to tell, and what sort of world and characters would you like to create? What skills would players need to excel at your game? And remember: the goal of any board game is to have fun, so let your imagination roam free, and be sure to follow it down any paths that look exciting. Adventure is just a roll of the dice away!

Issue Forty-Nine
KAT LEYH

Issue Forty-Nine Subscription DOZERDRAWS
Colors by MAARTA LAIHO

Issue Fifty KAT LEYH
SAD
50

Issue Fifty Subscription
VERONICA FISH

Issue Fifty-One
KAT LEYH

Issue Fifty-One Subscription DOZERDRAWS
Colors by MAARTA LAIHO

Issue Fifty-Two
KAT LEYH

Issue Fifty-Two Subscription DOZERDRAWS
Colors by MAARTA LAIHO

DISCOVER
ALL THE HITS

Lumberjanes
Noelle Stevenson, Shannon Watters, Grace Ellis, Brooklyn Allen, and Others
Volume 1: Beware the Kitten Holy
ISBN: 978-1-60886-687-8 | $14.99 US
Volume 2: Friendship to the Max
ISBN: 978-1-60886-737-0 | $14.99 US
Volume 3: A Terrible Plan
ISBN: 978-1-60886-803-2 | $14.99 US
Volume 4: Out of Time
ISBN: 978-1-60886-860-5 | $14.99 US
Volume 5: Band Together
ISBN: 978-1-60886-919-0 | $14.99 US

Giant Days
John Allison, Lissa Treiman, Max Sarin
Volume 1
ISBN: 978-1-60886-789-9 | $9.99 US
Volume 2
ISBN: 978-1-60886-804-9 | $14.99 US
Volume 3
ISBN: 978-1-60886-851-3 | $14.99 US

Jonesy
Sam Humphries, Caitlin Rose Boyle
Volume 1
ISBN: 978-1-60886-883-4 | $9.99 US
Volume 2
ISBN: 978-1-60886-999-2 | $14.99 US

Slam!
Pamela Ribon, Veronica Fish, Brittany Peer
Volume 1
ISBN: 978-1-68415-004-5 | $14.99 US

Goldie Vance
Hope Larson, Brittney Williams
Volume 1
ISBN: 978-1-60886-898-8 | $9.99 US
Volume 2
ISBN: 978-1-60886-974-9 | $14.99 US

The Backstagers
James Tynion IV, Rian Sygh
Volume 1
ISBN: 978-1-60886-993-0 | $14.99 US

Tyson Hesse's Diesel: Ignition
Tyson Hesse
ISBN: 978-1-60886-907-7 | $14.99 US

Coady & The Creepies
Liz Prince, Amanda Kirk, Hannah Fisher
ISBN: 978-1-68415-029-8 | $14.99 US

BOOM! BOX

AVAILABLE AT YOUR LOCAL COMICS SHOP AND BOOKSTORE
To find a comics shop in your area, visit www.comicshoplocator.com
WWW.**BOOM-STUDIOS**.COM